# Greasy Lips & Bacon Strips

"Love comes in many flavors"

-Bobby Donuts

**Ben** had quit his job as a janitor/cleaner. He wanted something better in life. Something less painful...he took a job as a used car salesman. It was a hot and dirty place and the pay was almost nothing but they had a fully stocked vending machine. Ben decided to take the job until his change jar was empty or he got fired.

Until then his only real purpose in life was to eat every snack, candy bar, and bag of salty chips in that vending machine.

Mr. Goodbar was the name of the car lot owner. Sam Goodbar, the only car lot that offers a fully stocked vending machine, he would often say. He was awfully happy about his dirty little car lot. It only had ten cars and half of then didn't run very well. One doesn't even work. He once was just a car salesman too, but now he owns a car lot. That meant everything to him. A greasy food truck came by at noon, this only made Sam happier.

**_Later that afternoon at the car lot..._**

"Excuse me." said the old women.

"Is this car for sale?"

"No." Ben said

Don't buy this car. Ben pointed.

"Are you busy?" she said.

"Yes, I'm very busy." Ben said

"What's wrong with the car?" the old women asked.

"Do you have a garden?"

"Yes." she said joyfully, clasping her hands and looking up to the sky smiling.

"That is what you should do with this car. Buy it. Fill it with dirt."

"Then...put it in your backyard and grow vegetables in it." Ben said

"If you're lucky a raccoon family might move into the trunk...just leave it open..." Ben waived his hand.

"It would then, as a car full of dirt, flower, vegetables and cute animals, actually have value." Ben said.

"That's a wonderful idea, I'll buy it." She said.

"I don't have very good credit." She said

"That's o.k.; we don't have very good cars.

### The next day at the car lot...

It had taken Mira awhile to get ready. She had on a tight black dress with white trim. What Mira wanted was a real man the kind of man that likes Aqua Velva, Pearl Jam, Bacon and blankets right out of the dryer.

When Mira arrived at the car lot she was large and gorgeous, wearing a black pair of sunglasses, a black choker, she had short black hair and 4 inch high black and turquoise heels... her boobs were so big she gave shade to small birds on the ground.

Today Mira was going to have a sexy-flirty-Saturday morning fun at the car lot.

"Then Ben saw Mira, He completely dropped his bag of corn chips. "Hi." Ben said, picking up his chips.

"Hello." replied Mira, walking slowly around Ben like a cat circling its prey...but for Ben she looked more like bacon wrapped around a chili dog. It got even more intense once Ben realized she was about to speak.

"I'm here to drive something strong." Mira said looking around the car lot.

"Are you here to buy a particular car?"

"A fast one" She said while getting a good look a Ben's butt and then getting side tracked from Ben's figure to the fully stocked vending machine behind him.

"Is that fully stocked?"

"...yeah." Ben said not really caring about the car.

"Ooohhh they have a lot of chocolate." Mira whispered to herself, now standing, looking into the vending machine. Ben seized the moment and with great anxiety and courage he said

"I have powdered mini-doughnuts." He said quietly, without much confidence. Not interested, Mira started walking away from Ben while eating her crisp chocolate Kit Kat. She was heading straight to Emilio Con Carne, the brother of Enrique Con Carne the Mall's food court janitor. He immediately started to comb his thick black greasy hair, adjusted his satin & polyester tie, corrected his posture and started to put his chimichonga away. Enrique was about to have Mira for lunch instead.

Ben was sweating now; he was short of breath and didn't know what to say. Mira was a sexy and forbidden woman of obvious great intelligence.

Ben then yelled the greatest best lie he could think of:

## *"My cat is going to die at 5 o'clock today!"*

*Mira and the sound of her black and turquoise colored 4 inch high heels came to a halt. She turned to Ben; she licked the Kit Kat chocolate off one finger and then after a brief pause said:*

*"Did you say cat... or... kitten?"*

"You, know, a cute kitten-cat." Ben said nervously.

"You poor thing." Mira softly said, moving closer to Ben.

"Ben doesn't have a kitten-cat does he?" she said in a whisper voice into his ear... "Yeah I do. It's at the shelter missing me." Ben continues to lie.

Ben and Mira went to the animal shelter. The sadness was overwhelming. The sad kitty eyes went on forever, cage after cage. The echoes of painful sad meows from dozens of stray cats were depressing.

"Here kitten-cat! Hey buddy...I love you."

Ben said fake crying.

"Do you see him?' Mira said holding Ben's hand.

"No." Ben said sadly...then

after a long and painful look for a cat he didn't even own, Ben squeezed Mira's hand gently lifted his hand and hers to a sad cat-kitten in the darkest of corners. Mira looked closely almost losing both

her eyes to an animal from hell as it hissed and swiped from inside the cage while she looked.

"Please give me my beautiful lost cat-kitten." he said to the attendant.

"I love this cat-kitten." Ben said putting his face up to the face of the dirty stray cat, the little beast kept biting and scratching Ben's bloody neck as they left the animal shelter.-

## Group Love & Weirdness

"You can start now..."

"Oh, o.k..."Hi,... I'm ...uh... I'm Ben... try to work out, eat right... go to the..... gym...I mean I eat junk food. from vending machines...my name is Ben Salami and I have a vending machine junk food problem.

"Hi Ben."

Hello, I am Mira Ricotta...I took something that wasn't mine...some stuff and things...

"What did you take?"

*10 pounds of delicious, hickory smoked bacon.*

**"NEXT..."**

Hey there everyone...I'm here because I won the World's Greatest Chili contest at the Chili and Beer Festival and they say I cheated...I did not."

"You did so; only Big Mama could make chili taste like that. Oh you know you stole my recipe!"

Trying to move on...

"...Anyway, my name is Enrique "Chili" Con Carne...I am the greatest chi con carne maker in the world.

"Hi Enrique" said the group.

"My name is Big Momma. I hit Enrique in the arm for stealing my secret chili recipe. The police called it Assault...as in ass...

"-uh boy...ok ....ok...let's simmer down and be nice.

The last but least member of our wonderful group is...

"Hello...my name is Emma Salisbury but everyone calls me Rooster. I stole some delicious BBQ chicken wings from Kentucky Fried Chicken...but that's not what got me in big trouble. After the girl wouldn't give me any more of those sweet but tangy BBQ sauce packets that you normally get anyway...right?, well I tried to jump over the counter like in the movies, ...but I was wearing my tight blue jeans, and they kept me from really jumping like I normally do...see and

I fell over the counter. So my leg goes flying... hits her in the face. I got scared cause she was gonna call the cops right, so I grabbed as much of that BBQ Chicken and as I could,

Because like this is it, right?! The law is after me! I'm on the RUN but I got BBQChicken! Right! Right!"

"So I ran into an alley and sat down in the corner out of sight and like...after I caught my breath, you know, I ate almost all of it..."

Oh my god...

Ok, ok everyone we have to get back on track. The court has ordered you all to my group therapy instead of having any charges brought against you....So with that said, My name is Dr.Michael Des Demona

Today we are here to talk about our

relationship issues with food

# Freshly Baked Brownies & A Ghost

Ben sat at his kitchen table thinking about what he could do.  He had lost his house keys. Ben got down onto the small apartment floor and began to look. With no luck he decided to try one push up since he was down on the floor.

At the age of 45, he tried one push up. He fell on his chest, hands out, gasping for breath, like a big fat fish out of water.

"One." he said out loud.

He did it again and fell again to the carpet gasping for air. The light around Ben slowly diminished and then everything went black for a moment.

A beautiful spirit woman named Pythia appeared. She was shimmering as if all the colors of the rainbow were contained within her. She had long white hair that floated slowly in the air like it was underwater. Her green and black dress floated slightly as she reached out to touch Ben. He felt her hand and it was like sunlight. A sweet smell of vanilla wafers and chocolate chip cookies filled the room as Ben's hallucination made contact with his skin.

"Ben." She whispered, while eating a freshly baked brownie.

"What?" he said, staring more at the brownie than at Pythia.

"You're fat." She said hovering above Ben a little,

"Ok...maybe I'm a little chubby." He said back.

*"You're going to die in 21 days."* She whispered softly with a cheek full of brownie.

"I'm working out." Ben mumbled in his defense.

"You must change." The Oracle of Delphi answered as a glass of cold milk appeared out of nowhere

"I will...I am...I do" Ben said in a whisper.

"Ben, also... your keys are on top of the refrigerator." She said after drinking the whole glass of cold milk and wiping mouth on her beautiful green dress...

"Thanks."Ben said...he was awake now. The beautiful Oracle of Delphi had gone the moment he opened his eyes. Later Ben went to the refrigerator to see if the keys were there....he found them. Stupid fat brownie eating fairy. Didn't even share. I hope I got more time than three weeks to live don't I??, Ben thought.

# The Dr. Is Mostly In But Sometimes Out...

THE PSYCHIATRIST OFFICE OF

DR. MICHAEL DES DEMONA

"Hello Ben. Have a seat." The receptionist said.

Ben took a little bottle out of his pocket and enjoyed a sip of alcohol.

"Cheers." Ben said as he lifted the drink. The receptionist buzzed

Dr. Des Demona again, insisting she see him quickly.

Ben offered her a sip and looking quickly down the hallway she grabbed the bottle and had a long drink of it. With a smile she handed it back, wiping her mouth quickly.

"My name is Brandy," she said.

"I'm Ben Salami.

The receptionist laughed at Ben as he told jokes.

"Ben...?"

"What are you drinking?" Dr. Des Demona looked at the black bottle.

"White Russian...why? Want some?"

"A bit maybe...." Ben smiled as he handed the bottle to the doctor. He wiped it clean and the doctor enjoyed a drink of it.

"That is very good...may I? ...........bit more?" Dr. Des Demona asked politely.

"Cheers, the good doctor said as he raised the bottle.

"Cheers to your journey." He said to Ben.

Ben nodded and sat down in the big comfortable black leather chair. Ben and the psychiatrist began talking for about thirty minutes, handing the black bottle back and forth, then Dr. Michael Des Demona said with a drunken whisper

"I was an ugly child…"

"No you weren't." Ben said as he took a sip…

"Yes. I was…

I was sooo ugly Ben…that they…in 4th grade, they didn't notify me it was school picture day. They said they did but they did not…"

Dr. Des Demona confided in Ben as they talked about childhoods. Ben quickly reassured him that it was because of his ugly childhood memories that he was such a great and empathetic doctor. As a beautiful child, empathy may have been a struggle to maintain from time to time. Ben talked about his childhood and child protective services, the foster parents and beating from a step dad... He talked to Michael about abuse, prison, murder, homelessness and hunger. Ben said to Michael that he was intrigued by math and art at an early age.

"I was stung by a nest of ground wasps as a 7 year old little boy. Luckily I closed my eyes real tight while they all stung me. My mom put ice cubes all over my face and her and friend rushed me to the emergency room. True story, I still have the pock marks on my face just below and above my eyes." Ben said

"So at age seven, your head was injected with wasp venom and you lived? That's incredible." Dr. Des Demona said taking a sip from the bottle...Then Ben got quiet and fixated on a ray sunlight that was shining through the window of the office.

"What is your occupation Ben?"

"I clean things."

"Shall we say a janitor then?"

"I don't like the term very much. I suggest cleaner."

"Why is that?" Michael said as he lifted the bottle to his lips.

"Cinderella." Ben said.

"Well she was always cleaning and Walt Disney never said she was a janitor that wanted to meet a rich guy. I mean she was but they called her a cleaner instead... all Snow White or Cinderella ever did was clean. She did maybe some laundry and she liked singing and whistling,

I do that too you know." Dr. Des Demona said laughing.

"I like to whistle in the shower, it echoes." Dr. Des Demona said in laughter.

Ben smiled, continued talking "...while I clean urinals, you know? Because it helps me not to look at the pubic hairs or urine..."

"Cinderella, she was always cleaning but secretly she wanted to party...she wanted some new clothes, nice shoes and a nice home...I want all that too! See how cleaners have happy ending but not janitors? So, no...I'm not a janitor, they never have happy ending....I'm a cleaner."

"What is a main concern you have Ben?' The doctor asked.

"That... we are out of booze." Ben said and held up the empty bottle

"Are you able to make friends? Or talk with co-workers?" the doctor said.

"I have a friend, Enrique "Chili" Con Carne.

"What is his business again?" Dr. Des Demona asked.

He's the janitor at the food court in the mall, he sells me used food." Ben said.

"I buy used food from him...or gently eaten as he says.  Also I would buy secret cleaning info and info about gross and disgusting stuff at the mall and food court and it's all at a great price. Usually for about $5.00...So you might say I'm connected in a way." Ben said proudly.

"I see." Michael said.

"I see that our time is up for today, Ben."

Will you look at that? It went by fast huh, doc?" Ben said.

"Be sure to schedule another appointment with the Brandy, I would like to talk with you more." The doctor said while finishing up some notes.

"I enjoyed the beverage you provided"...Dr. Des Demona said to Ben as he patted him on the back.

"Take care of yourself Ben, I'll see you again soon, ok? You have my phone number if you need to talk, just call me...Ok?

"Thanks."

Ben leaves the office.

# Ben Finds Food

Ben lived alone in a studio apartment. In this small apartment he had a broken futon, a kitchen table and two chairs. He had a small table with not much on it and when Ben opened the refrigerator; there was no food in it.

Ben opened the freezer; he grabbed three ice cubes for his Jack Daniels Whiskey and shut the freezer. He poured a small drink and layed down on the broken futon and thought about rainbows..snow... snowflakes... Every kind he could think of so he didn't have to think about the pain in his stomach from being hungry

Every day the breathing got harder for Ben. Every time he talked too much he would feel like he is going to die. The shortness of breath had increased recently. Every breathe he takes is one less breathe over all. Ben had no food in the kitchen and barely any air in his lungs. Ben thought of rainbows to help him fall asleep on his broken futon.

The next day Ben walked to the park. Ben was just as hungry as the pigeons he was looking at. The mall was located across the street from the park. The food court in the mall was such a happy place to be. Ben liked it because everyone was eating. It reminded Ben of a herd of buffalo sipping water or eating grass, somewhere in Africa. When people have enough food they are peaceful. Enrique always has food. Enrique Con Carne was the food court janitor. For extra money he sold secret information to Ben on who had the freshest used food or the cleanest bathrooms. He watched all the little restaurants in the food court. He knew everything about food. He had great used food from exotic restaurants like slightly eaten BBQ ribs from the Hawaiian Grill, left over broken cookies from the Sweet Spot or some pizza, all in one black trash bag.

"The Pizza Connection threw out good pizza, Ben." Enrique said, opening up a black garbage bag full of, broken, smashed pizza."

Ben raised two fingers up and looked around. Emilio reached in and grabbed a handful of two pepperoni pizza and gave it to Ben.

"The Wong Tong Palace has dirty oil and mice. They didn't change their cooking oil this morning."

He would quietly say to Ben as he emptied the garbage can near his table. Ben would slip him a $5.00

bill under the table. He would whisper the information. Emilio would lean closer.

"I need more info than that. What else you got Emilio?" Ben pressured him.

"Otherwise... I'll bid $2.00 for the pizza, not $5.00." Ben whispered, counting his loose change.

"Alright Ben, you're pressuring me man...how about...Phosphorus huh? What do you know about that? Did you know it was the 13th element to be discovered?  It is use in explosives, poisons and even  nerve agents and it's sometimes referred to as "the Devil's element".

*Spooky huh?*

It was the first element to be discovered that wasn't known since ancient times. It was discovered by

Hennig Brand in 1669. Brand was evaporating pee and produced a white element that glowed in the dark and burned brilliantly. This involved urine that was boiled down to like, a paste, then heated to a high temperature. A white and waxy stuff that glowed in the dark called Phosphorus was produced." Enrique Con Carne said.

"...We now know that as ammonium sodium hydrogen phosphate."

"Nice work ok ...Ok......BUT do you have any cookies?"

Enrique reached into the black garbage bag and found a pretty nice cookie with just a bit of Taco Bell sauce on it. Emilio apologized and tried to wipe it off.

"That's Ok...I like that, it's good. So Enrique handed Ben the Taco Bell cookie.

"It's a little too moist, I think it had some Mountain Dew spill on it. "It's good you should try it. Ben handed a little to Enrique.

"Not bad." He said, nodding his head with approval. Enrique turned to Ben and quietly said:

Also, don't use stall #3, men's lower level. Somebody vomited and I didn't really clean too well.

# A Kitten Cat Named Jimmy Dean

Ben named the cat-kitten Jimmy Dean, after his favorite sausage. He thought of the name while eating out with Mira. I-HOP was still open and they served just what Ben wanted. The menu had pictures of everything life should be lived for. It had strawberry pancakes topped with a caramel apple cinnamon sauce. It had French toast...eggs and steak bacon...hash browns and.... SAUSAGE!

"I am so hungry." Ben thought.

Ben straightened out his shirt and ordered with Mira who simply had a vegetarian omelet with dry wheat toast.

"Boring! Ben said... I can eat anything. In fact once I ate... I've-

Interrupting Bens rant she moved closer to Ben.

"So what is your full name?" Mira asks

"Ben Salami"

"And yours?" said Ben

"Mira Ricotta." She said.

..Like the cheese

"Yes, like the cheese."

Not knowing what else to say and getting nervous Ben says:

"I like French toast."

"Really? Some 15th-century English recipes call for "pan perdu" French for "lost or wasted bread", suggesting that the dish is a use for bread which has gone stale." Mira said.

The waitress set down the coffee, French toast, pancakes and sausage/ham and left.

"Give him some sausage." Mira whispered. The little cat started to purr and eat rapidly. He was starving. Ben gave it some ham. Then the waitress brought the rest of the food.

"I have an old bookstore." Mira said as she was reaching for the pepper.

"For how long?" Ben asked

"For about a year now, business is slowing down."

Mira looked at Ben and said in a competitive way:

"The thin crusted Italian tomato and cheese based pizza is called "Margherita" Mira said.

"The pizza is oven-baked flat bread commonly topped with meats, vegetables and condiments." Ben said right back to her with his eyes starting to squint.

Mira looked at Ben closely and took a sip of milk. Ben and Mira began to battle for knowledge supremacy.

"The term first appeared in 997 AD, in a Latin text from the southern

Italian town of Gaeta." Mira said smiling.

"The dough must be raised in wooded boxes at room temperature." Ben said.

"The pizza must be baked for 90 seconds exactly at 900 degrees...and when finished, the pizza should be held in the center and it should not fall." Mira said.

"I love all the different types of cheeses they use."

"It's a blend of three." Ben said.

"You know so much about food."

*"It's because I'm always hungry."* Said Ben.

# Ben's Bacon Soap

The next day Ben was doing the dishes in his apartment. Then something happened...Ben thought about it for a second. He felt a strange sexy effect come over him. Sweat began to pour from his hairy large chest. Ben had been doing the dishes. The bar soap that he used to wash his hands with fell into the big bacon grease bowl. The soap was covered with delicious bacon grease. It was still warm from breakfast.

It was like heaven only with bacon flavored bubbles... Ben quickly grabbed the bacon coated bar soap and went to the bathroom. The shower was hot and the steam was steamy. Ben's naked butt was pressed against the shower doors; bacon bubbles slowly gliding down his round chubby body as he smeared and lathered his naked body with bacon grease...Ben closed his eyes as the hot water pounded on his face. The smell of soap with bacon was more than he could stand. Clean, soft and relaxed, that was how Ben felt after the bacon soap shower.

## The Violation of the Delta Venus

Mira is an introverted bibliomaniac, often preferring the company of books over people. It was a beautiful day when Ben stopped by Mira's bookstore. As he walked in he noticed it was filled from top to bottom with books. There was no order to them. They got stacked as she bought them. She was a bibliophile that had gone over the edge. She was now a complete bibliomaniac.

Dirty little secrets were hidden among her books. About four books were hollowed out.

Mira had Hostess Mini white powder doughnuts stored in a book by Anis Nin's Delta of Venus.

She kept condoms in Henry Miller's Tropic of Cancer

and cigarettes in the Tower by Richard Martin Stern

and Jack Daniels in Charles Bukowski.

As he opened the old wooded door a small bell chimed.

"I'll be out in a few minutes, just look around a bit." Mira said as she put a huge stack of books into a box.

As he waited for her to come out from the stockroom,

Ben began to flip through a big book on her desk. Immediately it opened and it contained not words or phrases of wisdom but mini doughnuts instead. Out they fell. They just landed there after they rolled a bit, right under Ben's nose and within reach. She was going to be out at any moment. What should I do? He thought...he began to panic. Quickly, Ben shoved the package of mini doughnuts inside the crotch of his pants. He finished arranging his shirt and began to walk to the door. Mira walks out from the stockroom just as he puts his hand on the door knob

"Are you leaving? You are certainly impatient."

Mira said wiping a chandelier crystal clean.

"I got to go; I'll see you tomorrow, bye." Ben said.

The old door shut and the bell chime faded away. Mira sat down at her desk. Her eyes slowly looked around her desk. Something was different. She smelled bacon. She smelled doughnuts...sniff...she looked down at the book on her desk. The Delta of Venus was spread wide open...she had been violated. She looked at the book closer. Closer she looked and could see little greasy finger prints all over Anis Nin. Not even Henry Miller touches the Delta Venus in such a way.

She could smell the soapy bacon grease.

**"Ben." She thought.**

*"You little retard." She said out loud as she slammed the book shut.*

*"You stole my mini-doughnuts."*

**LATER THAT DAY**...It was quiet in the apartment. Ben was eating corn flakes with M&M's reading the newspaper when Mira called a few hours later. Mira had called and wanted to come over. There was a knock at his apartment door.

"So how are you?" Ben asked.

"I am well, thank you." She said as she walked in.

"Would you like a drink of some sort...Pepsi?"

"Yes, thank you." She said. Ben left to go to the refrigerator. Mira sniffed. She could smell the bacon.

Where it was coming from, she thought.

"May I use your bathroom?" Mira asked.

"It's down the hallway." Ben said.

Mira walked into the bathroom and immediately pushed the shower curtain away. Quickly, she looks for that delicious bar of bacon soap. She sniffed for the bacon soap. There it was half used but it didn't matter she grabbed it, wrapped it with toilet paper and put it in her purse. She flushed the toilet and walked out. Ben was walking back from the kitchen.

"Here you go." handing her the Pepsi.

"I'm not feeling good...I got to go, good-bye Ben."

Mira said as she was half way out of the door. She shut the door and she was gone. Ben felt a cold shiver. He went into the bathroom and saw the shower curtain had been violently push a side with complete disregard. It was gone, his secret was out -

*"Mira, you bitch...you stole my bacon soap."*

## Love Me Tender Mira, Like a Steak

Ben sat in the living room on his broken futon. After awhile, Ben started to think about red, thick and juicy meat. He was hungry for beef. It was primitive. A Stone Age desire was making his stomach grumble beneath his dirty T-shirt. He was getting dizzy from being hungry for too long. He had to eat soon.

"Eat is in the word meat...so is the word "me" So it is practically telling me to eat it." Ben was thinking to himself, standing in front of the meat section of the only food store in Sour City. The meat selection was increasing in price and shrinking in size and quality. Ben wanted a steak maybe a New York steak or a tender Filet Mignon.

None. New York Steak?

Zero. There was only one rib eye and a t-bone steak was left. Ben bought two steaks with the last of his money and walked back to his apartment.

It was a cold and windy night as he walked home. He saw a dog desperately sniffing a garbage can for anything edible. He needed to eat just like an animal to repair his own failing body. Ben felt sorry for the juicy cow he was about to eat. He felt bad for the starving skinny dog...Once Ben got home he gave Jimmy Dean, his cat, some raw meat. The meat was sustaining him and his cat. It was life giving amino acids.

"I'm sorry about this, I hope you understand." Ben said.

"All muscle tissue is very high in protein ok? Ben continued talking to the package of meat.

"I'm sorry cow, but I need to eat you."

"You contain all of the essential amino acids, and zinc. You have Vitamin B12, selenium, phosphorus, niacin, vitamin B6, a riboflavin and vitamin K" "Ok?"... So...into the frying pan you go.

Ben heard a knock at the door. It was Mira. She was in a hurry to come in.

"Hi! Ben!" She threw her arms around Ben and took off her coat

"Smells good!" she said excitedly.

"I have to turn off- oh just come into the kitchen, we'll talk in there." Ben said as he kept the steak from burning.

"Are you hungry?"

"Ravenous darling...she said playfully, while standing close to Ben looking at the steak.

"Yes, that is just perfect." Mira said.

"How are you?" she smiled.

"Good."

"...and where is the little kitten-cat?

"Sleeping"

Mira smiled as she looked at Ben finish cooking the steak.

"I only have Orange Fanta or Pepsi...If you want something nice to go with your steak I have pork skins. I would go with the **Pepsi**. *You should go with the Pepsi...*" Ben said nodding his head.

"The meat further back on the cow tends to be the best." Mira said

"Do you have any kind of sauce?" Mira asked.

"I have BBQ Mustard sauce packets from Arby's and two honey mustard packets from Kentucky Frie...KFC." Ben said nearly out of breath as he served her plate.

"That's fine." as she put some on her steak. "The BBQ mustard is actually good she said while licking a finger.

***"You're really smart." Mira said.***

**"Sorry." Said Ben.**

**"Don't be sorry for being smart."**

"Yeah... It's just most people don't like it. They get quiet and have nothing to say and it makes me feel like an outsider so I don't like to talk much usually."

"Yeah, I know what you mean." Mira said as she reached for some of Ben's orange Fanta.

## Of Mice and Men

The Next Day at 9:30 in the morning, in Bens Apartment

Knocking and rushing into Ben's apartment:

"I got these last night." Enrique said.

"Are these bagels any good?" Ben asked.

"They smell bad."  Ben said as he opened the black garbage bag.

"No way! He reached into the bag for one while Ben sat sniffing the air like a rescue dog trying to find a dead person.

"Yeah, I got them as soon as the skinny girl freaked out."

"Why did she freak out?" Ben asked.

I had put a dead mouse from the Wong Tong Palace into a serving tray of the Bagel Factory I tried not to laugh, really. She dropped the whole tray of bagels... into the trash... all grossed out... just because one dead mouse was in with the bagels." Enrique said as he ate a bagel almost laughing.

Ben just shook his head in shame as he licked the cream cheese.

"Now that is a shame to be scared to eat a bagel just because a dead mouse was on it for only a little while....

"So if you can do a mouse on a bagel...can you put a rat on a pizza for me? Ben said.

When?

Tonight maybe.

"What kind, because I have-"

"Hawaiian...yeah, extra ham. I really like that thin sliced ham."

Oh yeah, me too." Enrique said with big eyes.

I could put a few cockroaches in the baked potatoes...you want a baked potato?

Yeah! Ben got excited at the idea of large amounts of food on a daily basis.

Later that night, just as planned, the cockroaches and the rat were placed and the food was thrown away. As soon as it was..........there was Enrique Con Carne to empty the trash. Pizza, baked potatoes as ordered. It was great.

Enrique came over after work with a black bag full of trashy food. It smelled a bit and the methods got more extreme as time went by. "These hamburgers are great" Ben said.

He was able to get anything Ben wanted. If you want hamburgers Enrique just dropped an entire case of frozen meat paddies on a dirty grease floor.... They would call him in to clean up the mess and order him to dispose of the meat patties.

Next:

The Rooster's Tale &

# Eating My BBQ Sandwich Real Slow.

www.ingramcontent.com/pod-product-compliance
Lightning Source LLC
Chambersburg PA
CBHW071350130626
46556CB00005B/2112